Silverleaf Press Books are available exclusively through Independent Publishers Group.

For details write or telephone Independent Publishers Group, 814 North Franklin St. Chicago, IL 60610, (312) 337-0747

Silverleaf Press
8160 South Highland Drive
Sandy, Utah 84093

ISBN: 978-1-93439-300-0

Printed in the United States

THE Christmas Memory QUILT

My birthday is in June, when the air smells like suncreen and summer barbecues.

December is a long time away.

But on my birthday, Grandma brings a present
decked in holiday bows.

"Merry Christmas, Brynne," she says with a wink.

"What do you mean?" I ask.

Grandma nods toward the gift.

Merry Christmas

I snip the ribbons, tear the paper,
throw open the lid.

Christmas colors spill out of the
box in soft fabric patches.

"This is a birthday gift for you and a Christmas
present for someone else," Grandma says.

Mom blinks fast like she does when she
dices onions. Dad grins.

"Who?" I ask.

"A needy baby in a faraway country."

The fabric is for a blanket I will make
and donate to an orphanage.

Grandma will teach me to quilt,
and come Christmas morning,
a lonely child will be
swaddled in love.

"What a wonderful gift," Mom
says. Dad squeezes my shoulder.

I'm excited to quilt with Grandma, and I'm
happy that my blanket will comfort a
needy baby.

But I'm sad that the baby is lonely.

Sometimes I feel lonely too.

Each day I walk to Grandma's house.

We sit on the porch and sew, patch after patch, row after row.

My blanket is small
and simple.

Grandma watches
me quilt as she
works on a special
blanket of her own.

She begins a story
each time she threads her
needle, stitching family
memories into the fabric.

"I remember your mother's third
Christmas," she says.

Mom stood on tiptoes and pulled a bowl of
caramel popcorn off the table,
Grandma tells me.

"I found a sugary heap on the floor and a
very sticky three-year-old in the middle!"

She carefully sews a picture
of a popped corn kernel
on a flannel square.

Another day Grandma asks,
"Have I told you about my first
Christmas with Grandpa?"

I shake my head.

"We were too poor for presents, so
we walked around the church
yard gathering pine cones."

Grandma's eyes grow misty.

"For each one he found, he told me
something he loved about me."

She snips the thread as
she finishes the outline of
an evergreen tree.

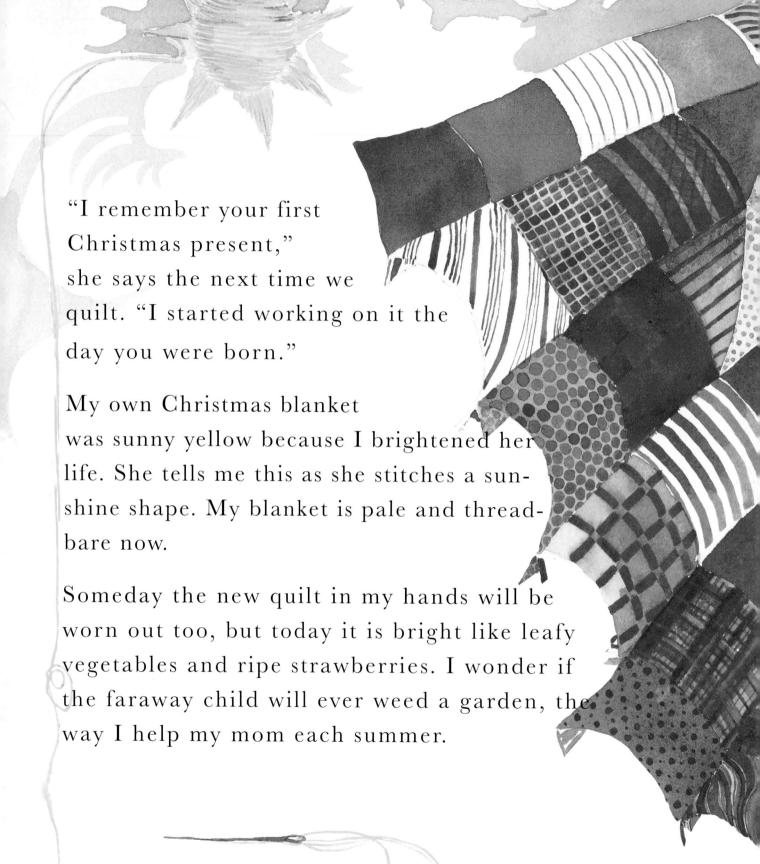

"I remember your first
Christmas present,"
she says the next time we
quilt. "I started working on it the
day you were born."

My own Christmas blanket
was sunny yellow because I brightened her
life. She tells me this as she stitches a sun-
shine shape. My blanket is pale and thread-
bare now.

Someday the new quilt in my hands will be
worn out too, but today it is bright like leafy
vegetables and ripe strawberries. I wonder if
the faraway child will ever weed a garden, the
way I help my mom each summer.

I skip to Grandma's house past dried cornstalks standing like skeletons. I want to make leaf piles and dive in, bake pumpkin seeds, and make wishes over a Thanksgiving turkey bone. I know just what I'd wish for—a brother or sister to play with me in autumn leaves.

When the weather grows colder, I leave snowy footprints all the way from school to Grandma's house.

I help Grandma set out her
nativity set and polish my favorite
piece, the baby in a manger. Then she
pulls out her needle and thread. She has
one more story to share. "I remember the
first Christmas," she says.

"What do you mean?"

She smiles. "I remember the baby born that Christmas
night long ago. I think of Him whenever I see your
happy eyes, whenever I see how much your parents
love you. He can make our joy last forever."

She speaks slowly, stitching a beautiful star into the fabric. Jesus was born in a stable beneath gleaming starlight. Angels sang. Shepherds bowed. Earth and heaven rejoiced. His mother wrapped him in swaddling clothes, holding Him close and singing lullabies. One day He would bleed in a garden and die on a cross. And then He would rise again—for us.

Her words feel like warm sunlight, like a soft Christmas quilt wrapping me in love. I think of the lonely child faraway and hope they feel warm too.

We finish our blankets two
weeks before Christmas.

Grandma puts mine
into a brown box,
ready to be shipped
far away.

She puts her blanket in another box.

"Someone special will enjoy this
quilt," she says.

I sigh. I'm a little sad to see
our memories go.

On Christmas morning, Grandma
comes early.

I find peanuts, an orange, and
chocolate mints in my stocking.

I find a doll and a sled beneath
the tree.

And I find a box wrapped in
Christmas colors, my name
printed across the top.

I snip the ribbons,
tear the paper,
throw open the lid.

I see soft fabric squares,
pictures stitched into them.

And I see a photograph
of a baby, his big brown
eyes staring up into mine.

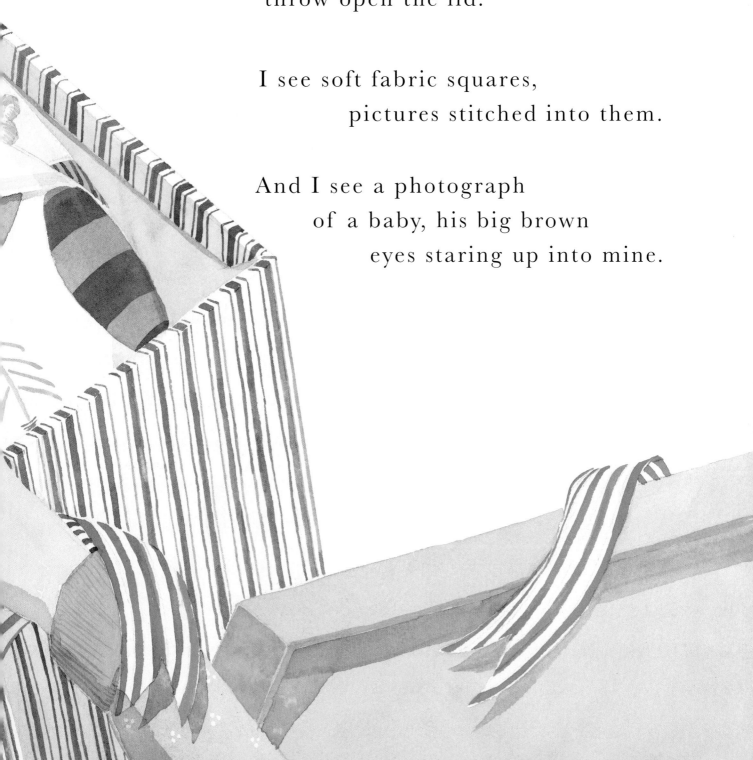

"Merry Christmas, Brynne," Grandma whispers, wrapping me in her Christmas quilt.

I stare at the photo, then look at Mom with questioning eyes. She blinks fast like she does when she dices onions. Dad grins. "Now you can remember and share our family memories," he says, "with your new brother." My mouth drops open, then spreads into a wide smile. This spring, a lonely child from a faraway country will come into our home. He won't be lonely anymore. Neither will I.

"Can we make him a Christmas quilt?" I ask Grandma.

"He already has one." Grandma says, pointing at the picture. I look closer at the smily baby and recognize familiar green and red fabrics. Now I know where she sent the first box.

When the house is dimmed to Christmas tree glow, I snuggle under my new quilt, dreaming of days to come.

My brother and I will weed the garden
and dive into leaf piles.

Grandma will thread her needle, telling us of
popcorn, pinecones, and the day my brother
came home.

She'll teach us of a silent, holy night,
and how our joy can last forever.

All year long, we'll carry Christmas
memories in our hearts.

Do you want to make a quilt like Brynne's? Ask an adult for help, and you can soon be on your way to your own Christmas Quilt!

You will need:
4 ½ yards of green scraps
6 yards of red scraps
⅓ yard brown
1 ¼ yard beige for interior border
1 ¼ yard green for exterior border
37 ½" x 43 ½" batting
Backing (This will also serve as your binding.)

Finished size:
37½" x 43½"

Cutting fabrics:
From the green scraps, cut:
• 40—3 ½" squares
• 9—3 ⅞" squares
From the red scraps, cut:
• 58—3 ½" squares
• 9—3 ⅞" squares
From the brown fabric, cut:
• 1—6 ½" square
From the beige fabric, cut:
• 2—1 ½" x 30 ½" strips
• 2—1 ½" x 38 ½" strips
From the green border fabric, cut:
• 2— 3" x 37 ½" strips
• 2—3" x 38 ½" strips

Instructions:

1. Cut each of the green 3 ⅞" squares in half diagonally. Do the same for the red 3 ⅞" squares.

2. Place a green triangle and a red triangle together, right sides facing each other. Sew up the longest side of the triangle with a ¼" seam. Do the same with the other green and red triangles.

3. Press the seam of the green and red squares you have just made with a hot iron towards the green side. This will prevent it from showing through the finished quilt.

4. Lay out the quilt squares in the design of the quilt.

5. Sew together the pieces in each row. Press the seams open flat.

6. Join rows together. Press seams all in the same direction. The quilt's center should measure 30 ½" by 36 ½" including seam allowances.

7. Sew the shorter beige strips to the top and bottom of the blanket. Press seams towards the red border.

8. Sew on the longer red strips to the sides of the quilt. Press seams towards the interior of the quilt. The quilt should now be 22 ½" by 29" including seam allowances.

9. Sew the shorter green strips to the sides of the quilt. Press seams towards the outside.

10. Sew the longer green strips to the top and bottom of the quilt. Press seams towards the outside.

11. Layer quilt top, batting, and backing. Leave 1" extra backing around the outside of the quilt.

12. Baste layers together. Quilt as desired.

13. Fold the extra 1" backing in half. Press. This will become your binding.

14. Fold the binding up around the front of the quilt. Sew ⅛" from inside edge of the binding to secure.